OLLIE'S TEAM
Plays
Biddy Baseball

OLLIE'S TEAM
Plays
Biddy Baseball

by Clem Philbrook

ILLUSTRATED BY FRANCIS CHAUNCY

HASTINGS HOUSE · PUBLISHERS

New York

Published simultaneously in Canada by
Saunders, of Toronto, Ltd. Don Mills, Ontario

SBN: 8038–5359–9

Library of Congress Catalog Card Number: 72–104748
Printed in the United States of America

To the Memory of Herb Brown,
Master Craftsman

CHAPTER ONE

Miss Carmody, the fifth grade teacher, sure was unpredictable, Ollie thought. You just never knew what she was going to do. Here it was the first thing Monday morning. They were hardly awake yet. So Miss Carmody was surprising them with a test.

But at least she was pleasant to look at, Ollie had to admit, with her wavy black hair, dark eyes and tanned face. Ollie did not wonder that his dad, a widower, found Miss Carmody pleasant to look at, too.

"Oliver, are you listening carefully to my directions?" Ollie suddenly heard a voice saying.

He sat up and folded his hands on the desk in his very best paying-attention manner. "Yes, Miss Carmody," he replied.

"Because that is exactly what this test is all about —listening carefully and following directions," Miss Carmody went on. "I realize it is spring, but some of you have not been very attentive lately. This test will separate the attention-payers from the daydreamers."

Would separate the girls from the boys, was more like it, Ollie thought disgustedly. Look at old Elmira Bisbee, would you? Elmira looked like a baby elephant topped with frizzy hair the color of rusty steel wool. She was sitting right up there listening eagerly to Miss Carmody's every last word.

And Deedee Miller was just like her, except she was slim and had straight black hair cut in bangs over a pretty, rosy-cheeked face.

Now her brother, Dusty Miller, was some different. He was tall and thin, with blond hair and blue eyes that were almost closed at the moment. You would never catch him listening eagerly to anyone's every last word. No, sir.

"Elmira and Edith will now pass out the tests," Miss Carmody said. "Please do not look at them until I tell you to. Then you will be timed. There are ten parts to the test. You will have five minutes to do them in."

Ten questions in five minutes. Ollie did some rapid mental arithmetic. This was two a minute you had to do. Boy, you couldn't drag your pencil much on this test!

With all in readiness, Miss Carmody gave them a final warning: "Now remember to follow directions exactly." She held up her wrist watch. "Ready now. Ten seconds—five—four—three—two—one—go!"

There was complete silence as everyone studied the test. Ollie glanced at his watch, too, then frowned at the test in deep concentration. He would just show Miss Carmody whether or not he could listen carefully and follow directions!

"1. Read everything carefully before doing anything," the test began. Only thirty seconds to do each part. Quickly Ollie skimmed down to the next one.

"2. Write your name in the upper left hand corner of this test."

Hastily Ollie scribbled his name as directed. That took about five seconds. Already he was way ahead. Gaining confidence, he went on to number three.

"3. Put a circle around the word 'test' in number two."

Two seconds at most. So far it was simple.

"4. At the bottom of this sheet, divide 1702 by 23."

Aha, getting a little sticky now, Ollie thought. It only took him twenty seconds to complete the division, though. He still thought the test was easy. And number five gave a big boost to his morale.

"5. When you get this far—the halfway point in

the test—please call out your name in a loud, clear voice."

It took Ollie about three seconds to sing out: "OLIVER SCRUGGS!"

The sound of his own voice startled Ollie and it suddenly came to him that he was the first one to call out his name. That could mean only one thing: he was ahead of everyone else on the test.

A quick glance around the room confirmed this. Elmira and Deedee were not so smart, after all. They just sat there like dummies, staring vacantly at their papers. Probably arithmetic had them stumped, Ollie thought. Bertha Long's Adam's apple was bobbing—a sure sign she was nervous. Dusty, chewing on his pencil, was watching Elmira and Deedee intently.

Bruce Dodge was, too. Bruce was the biggest and strongest boy in class, but he was certainly no scholar, Ollie knew. Bruce was a needler. He and Ollie got along like a porcupine did with Sir Winston, Ollie's English bulldog.

Ollie could not help smiling. If Dusty and Bruce wanted to watch somebody, they had better watch him. Elmira and Deedee had not yet called out their names.

All of this took no more than a couple of seconds, but it was more than enough to spur Ollie to even greater effort as he went on to number six.

"6. At the bottom of this sheet, multiply 97¾ by 3½."

In the interests of accuracy, Ollie allowed himself forty seconds for this one. After all, no one else had even called out his name yet. Reassured, Ollie went on to the next part.

"7. Put a square around the answer to number 6, and a circle around the square."

This was but the work of a moment, and Ollie plunged right into number eight.

"8. In a loud, clear voice, spell 'part' backward, without writing it down."

Spelling being Ollie's best subject, he disposed of this in short order. "T—R—A—P!" he spelled without hesitation. No one else had even reached number five! Jubilant, Ollie was ready for nine.

"9. If you feel you have followed *all* directions to the best of your ability, make the following statement out loud: 'Having followed *all* directions to the best of my ability, I am now ready for the final part."

With a song in his heart, Ollie recited number nine aloud and confidently faced the last item:

"10. Since you have read *everything carefully before doing anything,* complete only Part 1 and Part 2 of this test!"

It took a moment for this to register. Then Ollie felt like crawling into his desk and hiding. He had *done* it again! Instead of reading carefully and following directions, he had stepped right into a trap. Part 8! Trap! The test had even warned him.

With a sickly smile on his freckled face, he glanced around the room. It seemed that everyone was looking at him with a broad, smug grin on his face. So that's why Elmira and Deedee were sitting there like dummies! Following directions, they had skimmed the whole test before doing anything. Dusty, Bruce and the others must have taken their cue from Elmira and Deedee, Ollie guessed.

Copycats! At least he had figured things out for himself. Maybe Miss Carmody would give him an "A" for initiative.

What Miss Carmody gave him was another lecture. "Well, Oliver," she said, "Don't feel too badly about it. You are not the first student to be fooled by this test. Sometimes we have to be brought up short and stung just a bit to pay closer atention."

Ollie had to admit that it would be a long time before he forgot what had happened today. Whenever he was tempted to rush into something, he would remember this and be more cautious.

"After recess, we will start our unit on honeybees," Miss Carmody announced. "The hive came this morning. Then, at eleven-thirty, Chief Aldrich will speak on bicycle safety. He has a special announcement to make that will interest all bicycle owners."

Ollie was glad when the buzzer sounded for recess. Just for today, he would like to forget all about the test.

What was Chief Aldrich's special announcement? The boys were talking about this on the playground when Rod Little cornered them. The only thing little about Rod was his name. He was over six feet tall, with long arms that made him Willowdale High's star pitcher.

He also coached the Bulldogs of the Biddy Baseball League. The Biddy League was made up of farm teams of Willowdale's Tom Thumb League. In other words, if a player was not quite good enough to make the juvenile major leagues, he was sent to the minors for further seasoning. The Biddy League was the minors' organization.

"Some of you guys have been missing a lot of practice," Rod said. "But these same guys never fail to show up for the games, expecting to play."

Guilty glances were exchanged—especially by Ollie, Dusty and Bruce. They were three of the culprits.

"Starting with tomorrow's game, there'll be some changes made," Rod went on. "No practice, no play ball. There will be a short practice session at six o'clock tonight. Anyone who does not report will not be used in the game tomorrow. Are there any questions?"

There was one—a big one—Ollie knew, but he was not going to ask Rod. What if they did miss practice now and then? They were the best players on the team. Good enough so they were sure to go up to the Tom Thumb League next year. After all, the others needed practice more than they did.

When Rod had stalked off, they discussed his threat. Any coach wanted to win ball games more than anything else in the world, didn't he? Would Rod actually lose a ball game just to punish his best players? There was much speculation.

"He's bluffing," Bruce said.

"I think so, too," Dusty agreed.

"He can't win a game without us," stocky Billy Young said belligerently.

"So what are we going to do about it?" Ollie asked.

Bruce inspected his nails casually. "I, for one, am going to be watching that special 'World of Sports' program tonight at six o'clock."

"Hey, that's right!" Dusty agreed.

"Me, too," said Barney Sawyer, their lean first baseman.

Ollie hesitated for a moment. Lip curled into a sneer, Bruce pointed out, "If we're going to call Rod's bluff, either we hang together—or we hang separately."

"Okay," Ollie agreed.

The warning buzzer sent them back to the classroom. They were eager to start the unit on honeybees.

CHAPTER TWO

WHEN they were settled, Miss Carmody uncovered a large poster on the flannelboard at the front of the room. It showed three black bees of varying sizes against a background of red. At the left was a large bee with the word "queen" written underneath. In the middle was a smaller one labeled "drone." To the right was an even smaller one called "worker." On the table was an imitation hive with a cutaway removed, showing a cross section of the hive.

"Here is the material we have been waiting for," Miss Carmody said. "Since you should have completed the reading assignment by now, we are ready to begin our discussion of bees. Mr. Fuller has agreed to let us

make a field trip to his Honeybee Haven outside Willowdale so that we may watch the bees produce
honey."

There were excited murmurs at this announcement. Among other things, Mr. Fuller was famous for
his hard candy with a little pocket of honey in the
center.

"Maybe he'll give us some free samples," Dusty said,
rolling his blue eyes and licking his lips.

"Dusty Miller, don't you ever think of anything be-
sides your stomach?" Elmira asked tartly.

"None of your beeswax, Elmira Bisbee," Dusty retorted.

"Elmira Busybee!" Bruce kidded.

"That's enough," Miss Carmody said, tapping the
poster with her pointer. "On the left is the queen bee.
In a bee colony, there may be seventy or eighty thou-
sand bees—but there is only one queen. Who can tell
me why?"

Elmira's pudgy hand shot into the air. "Because
she destroys all the other queens," she said. "Just as
soon as she comes out of her cell, she finds all the un-
born queens and kills them with her stinger."

"How can she tell a queen's cell from the thou-
sands of others?" Miss Carmody questioned.

"They are larger and shaped differently," Elmira
replied.

Miss Carmody nodded. "Good, Elmira. I see you have been doing your homework on this unit." Pointing to the bee in the middle she said, "This is a drone. There are only a few of them in a hive. Can anyone tell me what a drone does?"

With a big grin on his face, Bruce waved his hand madly. "Nothing," he told Miss Carmody. "They don't do a bit of work. All they have to do is laze around the hive all day, taking life easy. They can't gather nectar because their tongues are shaped wrong for it. They can't make beeswax or royal jelly either. And they can't sting, so they don't have to take guard duty."

"What *are* they good for?" Ollie blurted out.

"To chase the queen up, up into the sky," Deedee informed him. "The one that catches the queen mates with her."

"Oh," Ollie said in a small voice, sliding down in his seat to make himself as inconspicuous as possible. Why couldn't he learn to keep his big mouth shut? Now Miss Carmody probably guessed that he had *not* done *his* homework.

Sure enough, she asked him the next question. "And here we have the worker bee," she said, indicating the smallest one of the three. "Oliver, would you please tell us what worker bees do."

Ollie gulped and tried to do some fast thinking. "They, uh—they work," he answered lamely.

Miss Carmody smiled. "Could you be more explicit?"

"He might if he knew what 'explicit' meant," Bruce butted in.

That took the heat off Ollie. For once he was glad that Bruce was a buttinsky. Miss Carmody turned to him. "Suppose *you* tell us, Bruce," she suggested.

Which did not faze Bruce a bit. "Well, for one thing, they feed the drones. They feed the queen, too, and build the honeycomb cells, and gather pollen and nectar. Then they take turns guarding the hive and chasing away any enemies." Finished, he smirked at Ollie.

Boy, Bruce sure had this down cold, Ollie had to admit. For some reason, bees must have appealed to him. Usually he was the worst goofer-offer in class.

Elmira had to get in the last word. "Another thing the worker bees do is air-condition the hive on hot days. If it got too hot the larvae would die and the wax cells would melt and then they would lose all their honey. So they bring water and put it all over the cells. Then they fan their wings at the entrance and this makes a breeze that cools the damp cells." Finished, *she* smirked at *Bruce*.

"Very good, both of you," Miss Carmody said. "Tomorrow we will examine the model of the hive so you can see the intricate arrangement of the honeycomb and pupa cells. But now we must end our talk for today. Chief Aldrich has just arrived to make his special announcement."

Everyone in the room had seen Chief Aldrich's shiny black cruiser pull into the yard. They kept close watch on all comings and goings out there.

What was the special announcement Miss Carmody kept mentioning? Ollie wondered. Chief Aldrich gave them a pep talk every spring. He always reminded them of the bicycle safety rules: observe all traffic regulations, traffic lights and stop signs; do not ride on sidewalks; keep to the right and stay in single file—*never* ride two or more abreast; be alert for cars stopping suddenly or car doors opening unexpectedly; yield the right of way to pedestrians; dismount in heavy traffic; use the proper hand signals when turning and stopping; do not ride anyone on your bike; have proper lights, brakes, tires and horn or bell.

These were all National Safety League rules of the road. Ollie knew them by heart.

He also knew that Chief Aldrich and his part-time assistant, Tom Drury, would set a date to inspect brakes, chain and guard, handlebars, wheels, reflector, seat and fenders. This was done every year, too. Only this year Ollie was worried about passing inspection.

His bicycle was missing one fender and his brakes were none too good.

"So I wonder what the special announcement will be?" Dusty's whisper echoed Ollie's thoughts.

They soon found out. Sure enough, the chief, a portly, ruddy-faced man, ran through the rules of the road, "to refresh your memories." He then showed a very interesting film. It was all about bicycles going on strike because their riders were not obeying the rules.

The riderless, talking bicycles ran away and gathered at the playground. When their owners found them, the bicycles aired their grievances. They told of rules that had been broken, and the unfortunate results. They refused to come back unless their owners promised to try hard to obey the National Safety League rules of the road. The owners all promised, hopped on their bikes and rode home, determined to keep their promises.

When the film came to an end and the lights went on, Ollie rubbed his eyes and looked around the classroom. The others were rubbing their eyes, too, and talking excitedly about the movie.

Miss Carmody led the enthusiastic applause that followed, while Chief Aldrich beamed proudly. It sure had been interesting, Ollie thought. He would never get on his bicycle now without half expecting it to speak up and blink its lights.

Then came Chief Aldrich's special announce
ment. "This year," he said, "we're going to have something brand new—a bicycle rodeo!"

"A bicycle rodeo! . . . Wow! . . . Hey, that
sounds great!" These were some of the comments that
greeted the chief's news. Ollie's personal reaction was
that it would be a lot of fun if you had a decent bike.
He guessed that he had better get busy and buy a new
fender and fix those brakes.

"The rodeo will be held a week from Wednesday
at two o'clock here in the school yard," the chief continued. "Bicycles will be inspected for mechanical defects. Then we will hold various events to test your riding skill. An oral exam on the safety rules will also be
given. The boys and girls who get the top five scores
will receive prizes. Everyone who enters will be given a
bicycle-training certificate. Now, are there any questions?"

Bruce had one. "What will my first prize be?" he
asked, with a challenging look around the room. His
fire-engine-red bike, with exclusive forward-thrust
tank design, split-second shifting and chrome-plated
parts, was the envy of all.

Ollie was in no position to argue with Bruce. As
he told Dusty on the way home, "I'll be lucky if that old
clunker of mine even passes inspection," he moaned.

"Me, too," Dusty said. His bike was no prize, either.

There was, however, one bright spot in Ollie's life. Sir Winston, his brindle English bulldog, was there at the end of his chain waiting for him when he got home —wriggling all over, whining eagerly, leaping up on him to lap a moist greeting.

It was at moments like this that Ollie realized the true meaning of the saying, "Dog is man's best friend."

CHAPTER THREE

Ollie and his father lived in a gray ranch-type house near the Willowdale Elementary School. It was so near that Ollie could see everything that went on over at the school and on the playground. The baseball field was right there, too. It was Ollie's idea of a great setup.

And Sir Winston was his idea of a great dog. Winnie was big and rugged, with bow legs and an underslung jaw. Although Sir Winston liked people of all ages, the same could not be said of his feelings about porcupines, skunks and other dogs. That was why he had to be kept tied up.

That was also why Ollie had decided to enroll Sir Winston in dog obedience school. "The Valley Kennel

Club is having a ten-week course in obedience," Chief
Aldrich had told Ollie. "Maybe if Sir Winston went to
school you could teach him not to run away and chase
porcupines and skunks and every other dog in town. It
might make life easier for all of us."

Ollie sighed. So far, it had made life harder for
him—and for Winnie. For one thing, the fifteen-dollar
tuition had made a big hole in his new-bicycle fund.
For another, all Winnie had learned so far was that
dog school was a heavenly place where he could chase
and bark at dozens of dogs of all sizes, shapes and ped-
igrees. When Winnie arrived for the weekly lesson,
there was usually chaos.

As Winnie was licking Ollie's face like a lollipop,
Mr. Scruggs drove into the yard. He stepped from the
car—a slim, blond young man with a smile on his face
and a twinkle in his blue eyes.

"I thought dogs should *never* be allowed to jump
up on people," he reminded Ollie.

He had attended obedience school a couple of
times and had heard Miss Hall, the instructor, repeat
this advice over and over again.

"Until they are broken of this habit," she always
added, "they will never learn anything."

"You're right, Dad," Ollie admitted. Firmly he
pushed Winnie down and went to get the training
manual and choke collar.

"This hurts me more than it does you," he told Sir Winston, slipping the nylon choke collar around Winnie's thick neck.

Mr. Scruggs winked as he went into the house. "That has a familiar ring. Now you know how I feel when I make *you* do something for your own good."

Before Ollie could give Winnie a lesson, Dusty stomped around the corner, hands jammed in his pockets.

"How come you're not eating an apple or a banana or a cookie?" Ollie asked him. "You sick or something?"

"Sick is right," Dusty grumbled. "I'm sick of that kid brother of mine. He went and cleaned out the frigidaire and the cookie jar. Not a bite of anything left until Mom comes back from shopping."

He jerked a thumb toward Ollie's house. "I don't suppose Mrs. Hunkins has any of her chocolate doughnuts left over?"

Ollie shook his head. "No such luck. I just tried her. She's going shopping, too."

Dusty grunted. "Boy, they're sending all that food abroad—and look at the starvation right here at home."

Before Ollie could comment, Dusty's brother, Wilfred, came trotting into view, bawling like a deserted calf. "I want you to wead to me, Duthty," he said, holding out a book. He was a skinny little five-year-old with jug-handle ears sticking out from under a mop of rusty-red hair. Since losing a front tooth, he had been having trouble with his speech.

"I'm sick and tired of weading—I mean reading—to you," Dusty said. "It's Deedee's turn."

Deedee, accompanied by Elmira, had arrived on the scene just in time to hear this. "It is not either my turn," Deedee declared. "I took care of him yesterday. Now it's your turn. Mom said so."

Bruce pedaled up to the curb at that moment and caught everyone's attention with his dazzling red bike with all its modern features. Bruce was well aware of their envy.

"How's that retarded mongrel of yours today?" he asked, looking scornfully at Sir Winston, who had curled up at Ollie's feet and was already snoring faintly.

"He is not a mongrel, Bruce Dodge," Deedee said indignantly. "He is a purebred English bulldog."

Ollie nodded proudly. "As purebred as the Prince of Wales. When he graduates from obedience school, I hope to show him some day."

"Show him what?" Dusty quipped.

"How to stay awake," Bruce jeered.

"You just wait, I'll bet he'll win all sorts of prizes," Elmira said.

"I bet he'll be an obedience school dropout," Bruce predicted.

Without a word, Ollie tugged Winnie to his feet with the choke collar. He would show Bruce Dodge how smart Winnie was! Grasping the leash in his right hand, he pushed down on Winnie's broad rump with his left. "Sit!" he commanded. According to the training manual, Winnie should sit.

Instead, he collapsed all at once, yawned and closed his eyes.

"What a moron!" Bruce scoffed.

Wilfred came over and tugged at the leash. "Let me do it, Ollie," he pleaded.

"If I can't make him, you certainly can't," Ollie said impatiently.

"From watching you, Wilfred has got this bee in his bonnet about being a famous dog trainer," Deedee said.

"You're telling me," Ollie said. "He tags us to obedience school every week. Hangs around and watches everything that goes on. I can't get rid of him."

"He's worse than the five-year-itch," Dusty observed.

"I think it's the seven-year-itch," Elmira corrected primly.

"Oh, no—that means we have another two years to go," Dusty groaned.

Ignoring them all, Wilfred stooped over and patted Winnie's wrinkled forehead. From his pocket he took a chocolate cookie and held it under Sir Winston's nose.

"Now I know where all the food is going," Dusty said.

Sir Winston opened one eye, then the other. Wilfred straightened up and Winnie got to his feet, pursuing the cookie upward.

A stern look came over Wilfred's face. "Thir Winthton—thit!" he commanded.

Licking his chops, Sir Winston sat.

"Thee!" Wilfred cried triumphantly, tossing the cookie to Winnie.

"He that—I mean sat!" Deedee exclaimed.

"Well, I'll be," Ollie exclaimed, scratching his head. "What does he have that I don't?"

"A lisp," Elmira said.

"Because of a missing front tooth," Bruce said, rubbing his hands together. "If you want to lose one too, I'll be happy to oblige."

Wilfred sat down on the steps to listen in on the conversation.

"No, it was the cookie," Ollie said thoughtfully, putting Winnie back on his chain. "To get a dog to do something, you have to reward him."

"Sure, just like me," Bruce said. "If parents want you to do something, they have to reward you, don't they?"

"Do they?" Dusty asked.

"Do they?" Elmira asked.

"Do they?" Ollie asked.

"Mine do," Bruce replied. "If you're good all the time, parents take it for granted and then they punish you when you're bad. But if you're bad most of the time, they're so tickled when you *are* good they reward you for it."

Deedee shook her head. "It would never work. Never in a million years."

"Make it a zillion," Dusty agreed.

"It *does* work!" Bruce retorted. "Who has the best bike in town? Who has more spending money than anyone else? Who gets to do what he wants most of the time?"

"Who?" Dusty asked.

Ollie sat down on the steps beside Wilfred. "Let's hear what he has to say. Dad told me you can learn something from everyone you meet."

"Even *Bruce*?" Dusty said incredulously.

"It works like this," Bruce explained, ignoring Dusty. "You've got to be helpless around the house. Ma asked me to help with the dishes just twice. I broke a dish both times and she hasn't asked me since. And every time Pa made me mow the lawn, the lawnmower wouldn't start or broke down or something, and now he doesn't ask me anymore. Says he'd rather do it himself."

Deedee was aghast. "Why, Bruce Dodge, you are a mean, selfish, deceitful, detestable boy!"

"Those are some of his good points," Dusty said dryly. "Now for some of his bad—"

Bruce was enjoying the shock waves he was creating. "And I also make sure Pa beats me up every morning," he informed them.

"I don't blame him," Dusty said. "If you were mine, I'd beat you up every morning, too."

"I mean he gets up at six-thirty," Bruce explained. "I don't get up until he pulls me out of bed. By then, all the chores are done, breakfast is ready, and I can take it easy."

Deedee pointed a finger at him accusingly. "You are nothing but a—a drone!"

Bruce was unruffled. "Why else do you think I knew all about bees? I could see right off we had a lot in common, drones and me. And you're all worker bees —busy, busy, *busy bees*."

Come to think of it, Ollie thought, Bruce always was watching from the sidelines while everyone else did the work.

"That's better than being a lazy old drone!" Dusty chimed in. "They don't lift a wing to help out."

"Why should they?" Bruce said. "They live off the fat of the hive. The worker bees are worn out in no time from all that work."

Deedee's wide-spaced brown eyes were moist. "I think that is so sad. The poor worker bees get so tired and weak the wind and rain beats them to the ground and they die."

"What's sad to me is they're so *dumb*," Bruce said. "The drones are the smart ones." He shrugged. "Me, I *like* being a drone."

Ollie had to admit that Bruce did less and had more than anyone else in town. The more Ollie thought over his own situation, the less he liked it. Mrs. Hunkins and his dad *did* take him for granted. He was a worker bee, all right—helping Mrs. Hunkins, running errands, doing all kinds of chores for his dad.

And what did it get him? A flat pocketbook and a broken-down old clunker of a bike with a missing fender and poor brakes!

Mrs. Hunkins came out on the porch just then. "Would you mind setting the table for me while I do a bit of shopping, Ollie?" she asked, with a big smile on her pink face.

She did not even wait for a reply; just hurried off down the street on her big, sturdy legs. She took it for granted he would set the table, Ollie thought dourly.

"I am *not* going to baseball practice!" he declared aloud.

Bruce nodded agreeably. "That's right. We are not going to practice—no matter what Rod Little says!"

Elmira and Deedee, the Bulldogs' faithful cheerleaders, were concerned about this. "What *did* he say?" Deedee asked.

"He said that if we did not come to practice tonight, we could not play in the game tomorrow," Dusty told her.

"But why don't you want to practice?" Deedee said.

Bruce winked at the others. "We're so good we don't need to practice, that's why."

"If you're so good, why are you in the farm league?" Elmira countered.

Bruce glowered. "We just needed a little seasoning, that's all. We'll make the regular Tom Thumb League next year."

"Rod knows it, too," Dusty said. "Don't worry, he'll use us. He's just bluffing."

Ollie thought so, too. After all, they had won their first six games. He did not believe Rod Little would break up a winning combination.

They would find out if he were bluffing tomorrow afternoon.

CHAPTER FOUR

THERE was a big, noisy crowd on hand for the game Tuesday night. Elmira was big—and Wilfred was noisy. Together with Deedee, they were the Bulldogs' sole supporters. Sir Winston did not count. Hitched to his post beside the bench, he had curled up and was taking a snooze.

"What did I tell you, Scruggs?" Bruce scoffed. "You had better show that dumb, bowlegged mutt—show him how to stay awake. As a mascot, he is a total loss!"

"Thir Winthton ith not dumb," Wilfred objected. "He ith thmart."

"Never mind picking on Winnie, Bruce Dodge," Elmira said reprovingly. "As a baseball player, you are nothing to cheer about."

Deedee clapped her hands together. She and Elmira were wearing their cheerleading outfits: white
pleated skirts and red sweaters. "Oh, that was a good
one, Elmira!" she cried. "Nothing to cheer about—get
it?"

"You've got it, all right," Dusty growled.

"And please take it away," Ollie suggested. "Can't
you see we have enough troubles already?"

Rod Little was out there warming up his starting
team. Ollie, Dusty and Bruce were warming the bench.
That was enough trouble for one afternoon, Ollie felt.

"I still think he's bluffing," Bruce muttered. "Don't
worry, when he gets in trouble, he'll call us."

The Bulldogs got in trouble the first inning. The
Pirates were not exactly a fearsome team. So far, they
had posted the league record of twelve consecutive
scoreless innings.

But their lead-off man, Chuck Andrews, indicated
that they were about to make up for it. Billy Young, the
stocky Bulldog starter, worked Chuck to a three-two
count. Then Chuck socked the next pitch into deep
center for a double. Rattled, Billy walked the second
man up—and the third. Already the bases were
loaded.

"Let's settle down out there," Rod called through
cupped hands. "Nothing to worry about, Billy, old
boy."

Apparently catcher Mike Turner thought differently. He walked out to the mound to slow Billy down. Everyone on the bench was shouting encouragement. Deedee and Elmira led Wilfred in a cheer: "Strawberry shortcake, huckleberry pie, V—I—C—T—O—R—Y; are we in it, well I guess, the Biddy Bulldogs are the best!"

Heartened by all the support, Billy stepped on the rubber, eyed the runners threateningly and delivered his pitch to Pirate batsman, Dan Fuller.

Ollie closed his eyes at the sound of the bat. It had that sharp, solid "crack!" that only a well-hit ball could give. When he opened his eyes, Larry Donovan was staring helplessly over the center field fence and Dan Fuller was crossing the plate. The Pirates were waiting in line to shake his hand.

"I bet Rod will put me in now," Dusty whispered.

"I bet he will, too," Ollie agreed.

Rod did look down the bench, and his glance came to rest on Dusty—briefly. Then he got up and went out to the mound. Billy scuffed at the ground as Rod talked to him. Then Rod gave him a pat on the shoulder and returned to the bench.

"Why doesn't he yank him before it's too late?" Ollie said. "Billy just doesn't have it today."

"Old Rod will come around," Bruce maintained. "You just wait and see."

They waited, and what they saw was more of the same. Billy did manage to fire a couple of strikes across the plate. Pirate shortstop Hal Ellis swung mightily at both of them and missed. But he whacked the third pitch over second for a single.

Dusty was gnawing on the end of a bat handle. "I sure would like to be in there," he said through clenched teeth. "I just know I could shut them off." He looked pleadingly at Rod Little.

Rod never took his eyes from the mound. He kept shouting encouragement, while Billy walked two more to fill the bases again. Still Rod did not make a move— not even with slugger Don Perry coming up.

Perry swung a pair of bats as he left the on-deck circle. He flipped one back and squared off in the box. He tapped the plate with the end of his bat, waggled it once toward the mound, then cocked it above his shoulder and waited.

The first pitch was in there and Perry swung at it ferociously. Ollie heard the satisfying "smack" of ball meeting mitt.

Billy worked Perry to a full count. Then Perry went for an outside pitch, fouling it off—a towering fly behind the plate.

Mike Turner tore off his mask and went looking for it. The trouble was, he looked in one direction and

it came down with a "thud" twenty feet away in another.

Ollie put his head in his hands and groaned. "We could have had one out! Boy, do I wish I were catching."

Rod looked calmly down the bench at him. "Any idea what Turner did wrong, Scruggs?" he asked.

"Yeah, he missed it," Bruce grunted.

Ollie knew what Mike had done wrong. Rod had told him about it only last week. "A righty will always foul an outside pitch to your right," Rod had said, when Ollie had misjudged a foul. "If it's inside, he will foul it to your left. Keep that in mind and you will always get the jump on the ball."

"It was an outside pitch," he told Rod. "He should have gone to his right."

Rod nodded. "Very good."

Ollie's heart thumped. Now maybe Rod would use him!

But Rod turned back to the mound—just in time to see Billy serve Perry a fat one.

The husky Pirate slugger timed his swing to perfection. Again Ollie cringed and closed his eyes. The same scene greeted him when he opened them; a grinning Pirate was crossing the plate as his teammates stood there with outstretched hands.

"Those guys are going to have awful sore hands tomorrow," Bruce said.

There was no joy on the Bulldog bench. Even the irrepressible Deedee and Elmira could find nothing to cheer about.

"How long is he going to leave Billy in there?" Dusty said, loud enough for Rod to hear him.

Until he got good and ready to take him out, Ollie decided. Rod let Billy face Teddy Nichols, the ninth Pirate batter of the first inning. The count went to one-and-one. Then Nichols hit a sizzling grounder to Herbie Snell at short. Just as Herbie grabbed for it, the ball took a bad hop and skidded through his legs into left field. By the time he retrieved it, Nichols was perched on first.

"I would have had that," Bruce boasted. "The dope ought to know enough to get behind the ball and keep his heels together!"

Rod looked at him with an amused smile on his tanned face. "Maybe if you came to practice once in a while, you could give him a few tips."

Then he stood up and surveyed the bench. Bruce, Dusty and Ollie looked at him eagerly. Now maybe he was going to relent, Ollie hoped. The game was fast getting out of hand. Their six-game winning streak was in danger of being broken.

But Rod crooked a finger at Les Martin. "Start warming up," he said. "Ollie, you can catch for him."

Then he went out to the mound. Billy was still protesting when Rod brought him in to the bench.

"No, Billy," Rod insisted, shaking his head, "you just don't have it today. Something is missing."

"Two baseballs, to be exact," Bruce pointed out.

"Aw, give me a chance, Rod," Billy persisted. "Chuck Andrews is next—and I almost struck him out the last time he came up this inning."

Rod might as well have left Billy in, Ollie decided as the game continued. Les Martin did not do any better. In fact, he gave up nine runs to Billy's eight before Rod relieved him.

It was a long afternoon for the bumbling Bulldogs. Ollie had never been so frustrated in his life. Surely, he kept thinking, Rod Little would weaken and use them to slow down the Pirates. When the score reached 39 to 0 in the sixth and final inning, he began to suspect that Rod had meant what he said.

Dusty, Bruce and he sat there on the bench glumly, long after the others had left. Even Wilfred had tired of the endless stream of Pirates crossing the plate and had gone home. Deedee and Elmira remained to harangue the dejected boys.

"Don't worry, he'll use us," Elmira mimicked

Dusty's prediction of yesterday. "He's just bluffing."

"Oh, shush and go away," Dusty said, without lifting his chin from his hands.

"My, they are so temperamental," Deedee clucked.

"Yes, ninety-nine percent temper and one percent mental," Elmira agreed.

"Me, I *like* being a drone," Deedee reminded Bruce.

"It's nice to have friends who stick by you," Bruce said.

"Oh, we're behind you one hundred percent," Deedee assured him.

"We just thought we would run through your faults, one by one by one by one," Elmira said.

Bruce turned and fixed her with his fiercest scowl. "Why don't you just run—period?"

Ollie sat unmoved by all of this. He was a great believer in taking first things first. The game was over. There was nothing they could do about it now. The sooner they forgot about it the better.

Elmira's remark reminded him of what Thomas Alva Edison had said, that genius was one percent inspiration and ninety-nine percent perspiration. That, in turn, reminded him of their social studies assignment. A week ago, they had been told to select a genius and make a study of him. On Monday, each of them was to name his choice and give his reason for making it. Ollie had not even thought of a genius yet, let alone make a study of him.

What was more, he was not going to fuss about it. He was a little tired of scurrying around being a worried old worker bee. Look how eager he had been in that test yesterday—and how it had boomeranged. Look how Mrs. Hunkins and his dad took him for granted. Look how mean Rod Little had been—just because they missed practice now and then.

From now on, Ollie decided, he was going to be more of a drone.

CHAPTER FIVE

THE "new" Ollie swung into action on Monday morning. Swung into *in*action was more like it, Ollie thought as he shut off the alarm and burrowed under the covers. Usually he was the first one up: he fed Winnie and hitched him outside; he set the table for Mrs. Hunkins; he brought in the morning paper and put it on the table at his dad's place.

But those days were over for awhile, Ollie thought drowsily, as he drifted back into sleep. At least until he gave Bruce's way of life a try—

"Oliverrr Scruggs, you get up this very instant—do you hear?"

The bedclothes were stripped back and Ollie

found himself staring up into the round, flushed face of Mrs. Hunkins. It was not jolly this morning. It was very stern.

"Is it time to get up?" Ollie yawned.

"It was time to get up an hour ago," Mrs. Hunkins informed him. "Now it's almost time to go to bed."

Ollie reached for the covers. "Okay, I think I'll stay right where I am."

Mrs. Hunkins yanked them away from him. "I think you'll get up and get dressed and march down those stairs, just as quick as you can," she told him. "You're already late for school. Winnie hasn't been fed and he's whining his head off. I was late getting breakfast on because the table wasn't set. Your father was ten minutes late starting for work, and he was out of sorts because he didn't have his morning paper, and— and it's all your fault, Oliver Scruggs!"

Ollie adopted an air of injured innocence. "All *my* fault? What did I do?"

"Nothing," Mrs. Hunkins sniffed. "Absolutely nothing. That's just the trouble."

All in all, it was quite a satisfactory start in his new role, Ollie decided. Nor did he bend over backwards for anyone at school. He did not even bend over frontwards. When Deedee dropped a set of flashcards, he pretended not to notice and she had to pick up every last one herself. Usually he would have leaped to her rescue and spent ten minutes crawling around on his hands and knees if necessary.

When Bertha Long asked him to help her with spelling because he was so good at it, he misspelled a couple of easy words on purpose and she went looking for someone else to help her.

That left Ollie free to do nothing but watch all the others scurrying around like—like worker bees! Bruce, too, was sprawled in his seat taking life easy. He caught Ollie's eye and held up a hand with thumb and forefinger joined. Ollie did likewise. The sign of the drones, he thought.

Even when Miss Carmody opened the discussion of geniuses, Ollie was relaxed. He was sure he would think of something when he was called on.

"To begin with, what is a genius?" Miss Carmody began. "What do they have in common?"

She went to the board and picked up a piece of chalk. "First, let's make our list of geniuses. Then we will discuss their qualifications. Bertha, let's start with you."

Bertha Long rose to her considerable height and cleared her throat. "William Shakespeare," she said nervously, Adam's apple bobbing.

"William Shakespeare," Miss Carmody repeated as she wrote the name on the board. "Fine. Yes, Elmira?"

"Albert Einstein," Elmira replied.

Miss Carmody wrote that one down, too. Then she looked at Ollie. "Who is yours, Oliver?"

It came to Ollie in a flash of inspiration. "My genius is a computer—an electronic brain," Ollie said. Miss Carmody knew that his father was a computer programmer.

"Dad claims that people use only a fraction of their mental powers," Ollie chattered on. "Even Albert Einstein used only about ten percent of his brains. Now you take a computer. It's not very bright, really. All it does is work with two numbers, 1 and 0. But it does it very well, using one hundred percent of its powers, never wasting any—"

"—Later, after we compile our list," Miss Carmody finally managed to break in. She then nodded at Deedee. "Yes, Edith?" she said. "Who is your genius?"

Deedee stood up and faced the class. "Elmira Bisbee!" she announced.

The room was filled with gasps, punctuated with a few scattered chuckles. Miss Carmody's hand hesitated only for a moment. Then she wrote the name on the board with a flourish. "Elmira Bisbee," she intoned.

Not to be outdone, Dusty popped to his feet next. "My genius is Ollie Scruggs," he said proudly. It was apparent that Dusty felt the honor of the boys was at stake. They could not be outdone by the girls—especially by Dusty's very own sister.

Even while he flushed with pleasure, Ollie secretly wondered what Dusty based his choice on. Ollie had been called a lot of things in his day, but genius was not among them. Nor did he think the class as a whole would greet his nomination with enthusiasm, in view of his performance in that test last week.

But Dusty managed to back up his choice very well a short time later, when qualifications were discussed. "For one thing, Ollie knows an awful lot about computers," Dusty pointed out. "And he is just about the best speller in the whole school, because he uses all these tricks to help him to remember words."

Deedee, however, made Ollie appear to be an idiot compared to her choice—Elmira. Among other things, she cited Elmira's brilliance in science.

Which Elmira proceeded to prove the very next period. Miss Carmody began a study in science class, comparing man's reflexes and instincts with those of lower animal forms.

"As an introduction to the unit," Miss Carmody said, "we will consider a few facts about stimulus and response. Take protozoa, for instance. These one-celled animals respond by instinct to the stimulus of heat and light by moving away from it or toward it.

Who can tell me what these responses are called?"

One hand only speared the air—Elmira's. "I don't mind it when she gets the answer before I do," Bruce muttered. "What bothers me is when she gets the *answer* before I even understand the *question!*"

"They are reflexes, or automatic responses," Elmira informed everyone.

Miss Carmody nodded. "Very good. And I know all of you have seen a common reflex action in human beings when your doctor has given you a physical examination. It is called the knee-jerk reflex. I want all of you to try this experiment yourselves."

She smiled. "This will be fun. Please choose partners. One of you may sit on your desk and cross one leg over the other. Your partner will then find the right spot just below the knee and hit it sharply with the edge of his hand. This will result in your leg leaping up automatically, with no conscious effort on your part."

There was a lot of milling around as they sought partners. Ollie got Bruce, who promptly hopped onto his desk and crossed his legs. Leave it to the old drone, Ollie thought. He never missed a chance to sit down on the job.

Careful to stand off to the side, Ollie prepared to whack Bruce's leg below the knee. Bruce's foot leaped up—just as Elmira waddled down the aisle—and caught her smartly in the backside.

Elmira gasped and drew herself up indignantly. "Bruce Dodge, you did that on purpose!" she declared.

Bruce was all innocence. "Why, Elmira, how could you accuse me of such a thing? I most certainly did not. We are testing knee reflexes, aren't we? I just happen to have extra good reflexes, that's all."

Ollie could not help but smile as a pouting Elmira waddled on her way. Bruce's reflexes sure were *extra* good. So good, in fact, that Bruce's foot had leaped up *before* Ollie even had a chance to hit his leg.

CHAPTER SIX

BRUCE demonstrated his reflexes again at the bicycle rodeo on Wednesday. But it was Ollie who started things off with a bang—or a crash, to be more exact. Two lines, boys and girls, were formed facing Chief Aldrich and Tom Drury, the two inspectors. The men stood beside two separate card tables some distance away, ready to inspect the bicycles. Rod Little and Mr. Waterhouse, the principal, sat at the card tables. It would be their jobs to check off the inspection forms for Chief Aldrich and Tom Drury.

Mr. Waterhouse was a tall, handsome man with wavy white hair. Seeing Nosy Newman, bespectacled reporter for the weekly *Courier*, standing by with a camera, Mr. Waterhouse ran a comb through his hair and straightened his tie.

"Here is the idea," Chief Aldrich began. "When we call out 'next,' the person at the head of the line pedals toward us at a good clip. When we say 'brakes,' you are to apply your brakes immediately. Then you will present the inspection form we have passed out to you to Mr. Waterhouse and Rod Little."

Ollie suddenly remembered with a pang of annoyance that he had neglected to get his brakes fixed and buy a new fender. There was nothing he could do about the fender at this late date. If he came down on his brakes extra hard, however, he thought they would work all right.

"Tom Drury and I will inspect your brakes, handlebars, wheels, seat, reflector, fenders, and so forth," the chief went on. "Mr. Waterhouse and Rod will either check them off as okay, or note any defects that should be corrected. Ready now—Elmira and Bruce, you start it off."

Elmira on a bicycle was like a big bullfrog on a little lily pad—she lopped over so the bicycle could hardly be seen. But she did manage to get down there quite fast and brake to a stop without incident.

Bruce was first in the boys' line. "You might know old Dodge would be at the head of the line," Dusty grumbled. "He has to go and show everyone up."

Bruce did, too. He took off like a jet on his gleaming bike and came to a pinpoint stop on command. Inspecting his bike for defects was a mere formality.

"The only thing defective on his bike is him," Dusty sniffed.

"Okay, Little Ollie, you're next," Chief Aldrich called.

Not to be outdone by Bruce, Ollie took off like a jet, too. But he did not come to a pinpoint stop on command.

"Brakes!" Chief Aldrich sang out.

Ollie came down on the brakes, but they did not hold. He kept on going—right into the card table, behind which sat Mr. Waterhouse. The next thing Ollie knew, Mr. Waterhouse was lying flat on his back on the ground, with the card table upside down on top of him. Ollie was on top of the card table. His bicycle was on top of him. Mr. Waterhouse looked as though he had been caught in a tornado.

When order was finally restored, Chief Aldrich took Ollie's inspection form and handed it to Mr. Waterhouse. "Defective brakes," he said gravely.

"Yes, I know," Mr. Waterhouse replied ruefully, as he made the notation.

Ollie did not exactly distinguish himself in the first event of the rodeo either. Two rows of empty cans, placed about two feet apart, formed a serpentine route. "This is sort of like running a slalom course," Chief Aldrich told them. "You are to take turns riding between the rows of cans. For every can you knock over, you lose two points."

Again, Bruce got in line first. And again, he took off like a jet—whizzing down the twisting aisle of cans and out the other end without even ticking a single one.

"It's that snazzy bike of his," Dusty said with a shrug. "How can you beat him?"

"We can't," Ollie said dejectedly. "There's no point in trying."

"That's not the spirit," Elmira scolded them. "You have to think positive."

"We are," Dusty said practically. "We're positive Bruce is going to beat us."

"Look at the bike he has," Ollie pointed out.

"Look at the bike *I* have," Deedee said. "It is just as old as yours, Oliver Scruggs. But I do not sit around like an old drone moaning about it. I take good care of it."

"There was absolutely no excuse for your brakes not being fixed," Elmira added.

In the very next event, Ollie had further cause to regret this defect. A narrow piece of white tape was placed on the blacktop. "The object here is to ride toward the tape and come to a stop right on top of it, if you can," Chief Aldrich explained. "You will lose two points for every inch you go past, or fall short of the

tape. Rod will do the measuring. This is a good test of your timing and reflexes."

Bruce smirked at Elmira. "Guess who's going to win this? We already know my reflexes are extra good, don't we?"

He then stopped smack dab on the tape. "Dead center," Rod praised him.

Because of his poor brakes, Ollie almost ran into the field. He went eighteen inches past the tape. Rod clucked and shook his head. "Too bad, Scruggs. That will cost you thirty-six points."

Dusty was overanxious and stopped eight inches short. Elmira and Deedee both came within three inches of the tape.

"So where did your positive thinking get you?" Dusty asked Deedee.

"Five inches closer than you, smarty," Deedee replied airily.

In the final event, riding a figure eight pattern in a restricted space, Bruce handled his bike to perfection.

"Let's hope he flunks the oral test," Dusty told Ollie. "That's the only way he can lose."

But Bruce got a hundred in the oral test. Combined with his riding skill, this earned him first place for the boys—a silver cup. Deedee edged out a surprisingly agile Elmira for first prize in the girls' competition.

"If you worked at it a little harder," Deedee lectured Dusty and Ollie, "*you* might be winners, too."

Ollie disagreed. He had tried as hard as anyone, yet his day had been a complete disaster. No, he was still too much of a worker bee. Look who had won the rodeo—the biggest drone in school.

Ollie was not surprised when Rod Little approached Dusty, Bruce and him after the rodeo. "Don't forget baseball practice tonight at six," he reminded them. "No practice, no play ball on Friday."

Ollie looked at Dusty after Rod left. "Do you still think he's bluffing?" he asked.

Dusty shrugged. "Ah, don't worry about him. I know just how to handle him now. There's only one way to get along with Rod Little."

"How?" Ollie said.

"How?" Bruce said.

"Simple," Dusty replied. "We do what he says. We go to practice."

CHAPTER SEVEN

BRUCE'S victory in the rodeo was very much on Ollie's mind when he got home from school. What a drone Bruce was! Yet everything seemed to fall his way.

"You've got to be helpless around the house," Bruce had said. This bit of advice echoed in Ollie's mind as he wheeled the lawnmower out of the garage. Rebellion churned in him at the thought of the ballgame that was being televised. Why should he be a worker bee all the time? Why not be a drone for a change? After a halfhearted attempt to start the mower, he decided to watch the game.

"I couldn't get the lawnmower started," he told his father at supper—failing to add that he had not tried very hard.

"Never mind, I'll do it myself," Mr. Scruggs said cheerily. "I've been sitting all day and could use some exercise. You can help Mrs. Hunkins with the dishes."

Ollie helped Mrs. Hunkins for about two minutes —or two dishes, to be exact. Two broken dishes that he dropped—accidentally. When the second one hit the floor, Mrs. Hunkins snatched the dishcloth and shooed him out of the kitchen.

"Land sakes alive, I can't afford to have you help me," she scolded. "Now get along to baseball practice —scat!"

Ollie went along to baseball practice, where he and Bruce watched the worker bees run all over the place, chasing fly balls and grounders. Unless a ball came down right where they stood, he and Bruce let it fall to the ground, unmolested. They intended to save their energy for a real game.

Nor did they extend themselves at the plate. If the ball was not exactly where they liked it, they let it go. They both struck out three times in a row.

"Ollie bats like Ruth," Deedee commented to Elmira, when Ollie slunk back to the bench after his third strikeout.

"That shows how much you know about base-ball," Dusty scoffed. "Babe Ruth was one of the greatest hitters who ever lived."

Deedee giggled. "Who said anything about *Babe*

Ruth? I'm talking about Ruth Bagley, who plays soft-ball on our team and never gets a hit."

"If Ollie and Bruce played on our team, we'd trade them," Elmira said.

Bruce grunted. "If I had to play on your team, I'd want to be traded."

After one strikeout, Dusty fared a little better his next time up. "Your left foot is in the wrong position," Rod Little advised him, after he missed a couple of good ones.

"So is his right," Bruce quipped. "Both of them should be over here beside the bench."

Ignoring Bruce, Rod came over, borrowed Dusty's bat and took his stance at the plate. "Relax," he said to Dusty. "You're treading around as if you were standing on live coals. Now watch me."

He waved his bat just twice, while Billy Young looked him over. But the moment Billy went into his windup, Rod cocked his bat and froze, rigid as a statue. The ball came in belt high and he stepped into it with a fluid, level swing, stroking a single into left field.

"That's all there is to it," he told Dusty. "Wag your bat and move around all you want to, if it helps to get loose. But once the pitcher winds up, relax physically and concentrate on *watching that ball*."

Dusty wet his lips and stepped back into the box;

feet planted the width of his shoulders, square to the plate, weight on the balls of his feet.

He waggled the bat once, then cocked it. Nor did he shift his feet or waggle the bat again—even with Billy glaring at him from out there on the mound. Instead, Dusty stared impassively back, waiting and watching.

It was a duplicate of Rod's performance. Dusty met the ball just in front of the plate, with arms extended and good wrist action. It was another clean single into left field.

Rod nodded approvingly. "You catch on fast," he said.

"Lucky," Dusty replied, but he seemed pleased.

"Know-how," Rod corrected. "Know-how, and practice." He glanced significantly at Ollie and Bruce. "That's what separates a winner from a loser."

Dusty distinguished himself further by performing well on the mound. Ollie and Bruce, on the other hand, were still as unspectacular afield as they had been at the plate.

Bruce did some pitching, too. With Mike Turner dancing off first, Bruce took a full windup and Mike stole second.

"You know better than that, Dodge," Rod warned him. "Never take a windup with anyone on base. Use a sideward stance, facing third base, with your head turned enough to keep tabs on the runner."

Bruce proceeded to repeat his mistake—taking a full windup. Mike slid into third with his second stolen base in a row. Then Bruce wound up again—on the bench.

Ollie did not do much better. When he was not catching, sometimes he was used in right field. First, he caught a high fly in foul territory with a man on third. "Just a reminder, Scruggs," Rod told him. "In a real game, never, I mean *never*, catch a long foul late in a game with the winning or tying run on third and less than two out."

Next, Ollie lost a ball in the sun. Larry Donovan finally found it—after two men had crossed the plate. Then Ollie started making basket catches down around his belt buckle.

"Lay off the grandstanding," Rod warned him. "Hold your glove up there where you can follow the ball into it."

On the next fly ball to right field, Ollie held his glove up there, but he did not follow the ball into it. The ball beaned him while he was circling aimlessly under it.

"It's a good thing the ball hit you on the head," Bruce sympathized when Ollie came in to the bench.

"If it had hit you anywhere else, you could have been hurt."

All things considered, Dusty felt qualified to lecture Ollie on the way home. "You didn't put yourself out much today," he said. "You're getting as bad as Bruce. You'll never stay on the team if you don't get on the ball."

"On the ball—hey, that's not bad," Ollie replied. But he was too relaxed to care about the baseball team, one way or the other. When he got home and Winnie jumped all over him again, he hugged his pet and let him lick away.

"Dogs should *never* be allowed to jump up on people."

Again Miss Hall's advice sounded faintly in Ollie's mind. So faintly that he could barely hear it. He was beginning to like this carefree life where everyone else did all the work—and all the worrying.

"I guess you can be a drone, too, if you want to be," he said aloud to Winnie. "It's a lot easier than being a worker bee."

"That's one way to look at it," said a voice in the gathering gloom. Startled, Ollie looked all around, but could see no one. Then his glance came to rest on his bicycle, leaning against the porch steps. He remembered those talking bicycles in the film on bicycle safety. Ollie swallowed uneasily. Was it possible—

"But don't forget that there is another side to the story," the voice went on. Then Ollie saw his father standing there behind the screen door.

"Oh, hi, Dad," he said in relief. "I thought I was hearing things."

"You were," Mr. Scruggs said, coming out on the porch. "I was about to point out that drones have their place, but it's the worker bees who get things done." Smiling, he looked at their snug home. "No worker bees—no hive."

"No worker bees—no honey," added another voice. They both turned to see Mrs. Hunkins standing in the doorway. "If you gentlemen are interested," she went on, "I just happen to have some fresh strawberry shortcake and whipped cream."

They were interested. But even when Ollie started his second helping, he still thought that Winnie could be a drone if he wanted to be. Ollie was finding it to be an interesting change from his former way of life. Oh, he had caught himself several times feeling that he should get up on time and feed and discipline Winnie and set the table and wipe the dishes and get his dad's paper and mow the lawn. If he did not watch himself very carefully, he was apt to fall right back into his same old good habits.

But with diligence he was learning to break them, one by one. And everything got done, just the same. Mrs. Hunkins set the table and did the dishes and fed Winnie. His dad got his own paper and mowed the lawn.

And Winnie was no worse in obedience training. No better—but no worse. The only reason Ollie made the effort to take Winnie to obedience school any more was because he had paid in full for the course and it was not refundable.

The next lesson was tomorrow night, and they would be there. Ollie was determined to get his money's worth.

CHAPTER EIGHT

I T WAS a lively session the following evening. When weather permitted, obedience school was held outside the armory in the big parking lot. Ollie was the last to arrive, as usual—with Wilfred tagging along, pestering Ollie to let him handle Winnie.

When Ollie got there, the dogs and their masters were already lined up, facing ramrod-straight Miss Hall, the instructor.

Ollie tried to sneak into the end of the line as inconspicuously as possible. This was not easy because Spooky, a brown and white terrier, had to go and yap at Winnie.

It was too much to ask of Winnie not to bark

back, which he promptly did. Half the other dogs
joined in the chorus. It was like a single domino upset-
ting a whole line of dominoes. In no time at all, what
had been an orderly, silent row of dogs was turned
into a howling, snapping, baying, growling, ki-yiing
mob of yippies.

Above the bedlam could be heard Miss Hall's
calm, forceful voice commanding, "Sit your dogs!"

In due time they all sat, except Sir Winston. He
stretched out on the warm asphalt, yawned once, put
his head between his paws and closed his eyes.

With Wilfred banished to the sidelines, Miss Hall
did a left face and marched stiff as a toy soldier over to
stand in front of Ollie and Sir Winston.

"As I have said, half the battle is in training the
handler to handle the dog properly," she told everyone.

Yes, she had said that—a dozen times, at least,
Ollie recalled.

"We can no more blame an unruly dog than we
can blame an unruly child," Miss Hall went on. "Both
are a product of a too-permissive environment."

She stepped forward and reached for the leash in
Ollie's hand. "May I?" she said—although it was not so
much a request as a command.

Meekly Ollie handed her the leash.

"Come, Sir Winston!" Miss Hall commanded,
pulling smartly on the leash.

Sir Winston came. Came to, that is. Opening one bloodshot eye, he blinked at her resentfully.

Again she pulled on the leash. This time Winnie obliged by scrambling to his feet.

"Come, Sir Winston!" Miss Hall repeated, reeling him to her, hand over hand on the leash, like a struggling fish.

"Heel!" Miss Hall ordered. At the same time she pulled Winnie to her left side, jerked back on the leash and held him in proper position. The nylon choke collar was doing its work.

"Sit!" she told him. Pulling up on the leash with her right hand, she pushed down hard on Winnie's rump with her left hand. Ollie cringed as the choke collar tightened on Winnie's thick neck. Winnie sat, however—a bit crooked, but he sat.

Next, Miss Hall dropped to one knee and ordered him to "down" in a voice that descended in pitch. At the same time, she pulled straight down on the leash with her right hand, helping Winnie along a bit by knocking his front legs out from under him. Winnie went down with a grunt. Planting her left foot on the leash to hold him down, Miss Hall told Winnie to "stay" as she rose to her feet.

"Now we see what a firm hand can do," Miss Hall told everyone. "Many people—" and here she looked reprovingly at Ollie—"many people think the choke collar is an instrument of torture. Actually, it is a very humane way of controlling a dog, just as the bit in a horse's mouth teaches and controls a horse."

She smiled all around. "So much for the physical method of teaching your dog. Now we must realize that all dogs want to please their masters. Knowing this, we have only to adopt an 'attitude of command' to have our dogs 'eating out of our hands.' This is far better than having them 'bite the hand that feeds them'— isn't it?"

Miss Hall smiled at her own cleverness. Then she sobered, adopting her "attitude of command," Ollie guessed.

"Please watch closely," she added. "Note the confidence in my tone as I order Sir Winston to stay 'down' and leave him."

Coming to full attention, she fixed Winnie with her firmest glance and repeated "down."

There was a hushed silence as Miss Hall then backed away cautiously and dropped the leash to the ground in front of Winnie's nose—all the while watching him closely.

"I will now circle him twice," Miss Hall alerted the class. "See how he responds to my 'attitude of command.' "

What Ollie saw as Miss Hall then marched around Winnie twice was that Winnie actually was not responding to anything—he had closed his eyes blissfully and gone to sleep.

Completing her tour, Miss Hall leaned over, picked up the end of the leash and straightened. "And that," she said smugly, "is how we—"

She was interrupted in mid-sentence by the unmistakable sound of snoring: deep, even, loud snoring. Tittering could be heard along the length of the line. Tightlipped, Miss Hall handed the leash to Ollie, did an about-face and returned to her position facing the center of the line.

"We will now practice heeling," she announced, as though nothing had happened. "Everybody right—face! Start your dog from a sitting position. When I give the signal, proceed in a normal walk around the parking lot. If your dog gets ahead of you, say 'heel' and jerk back on the leash, tightening the choke collar. When he drops back to the proper position at your left side, ease up on the leash. By now, you should not have to drag your dog—nor should he be dragging you."

Miss Hall held up a finger. "When the exercise is finished, reward your dog with praise. Remember that dogs are like children. Both like to have their efforts appreciated."

Given his head, Winnie lunged for Spooky, the sassy terrier. Spooky tried to hide behind his master, wrapping the leash firmly around his master's legs.

Again a chain reaction followed, with dogs breaking ranks in all directions. There was baying and barking and bedlam. When everything was calm again, Miss Hall addressed Ollie.

"Please take Sir Winston around the corner and give him a private lesson, Oliver," she said. "When school is over, I would like to talk with you."

When obedience school was dismissed, and the others had left, Ollie emerged from around the corner with Winnie and Wilfred at his heels. Miss Hall was standing by her blue station wagon waiting for him.

"I am disappointed in you, Oliver," she greeted him. "You have a fine English bulldog in Sir Winston. With a little training and discipline, he could become a show dog of championship caliber."

"Thir Winthton ith thmart," Wilfred piped up.

Ollie grinned proudly. "Do you really think so, Miss Hall?" he asked.

Miss Hall nodded. "I really think so," she replied. "But he will never realize his potential unless you help him. For a while you were trying and Sir Winston made progress, but lately you seem to have given up all effort to train him."

Solemn as an owl, Wilfred stood there taking this all in.

Ollie hung his head and scuffed at a stone. "I—I

just can't use the choke collar on him. I don't want to hurt him."

Miss Hall smiled. "We all need a choke collar, Oliver—something that brings us up short and draws our attention to things we are doing wrong," she said gently. "Think it over and I'm sure you'll agree."

Ollie thought it over all the way home. But no matter how hard he tried, he could not agree with Miss Hall. "As far as I'm concerned," he told Wilfred, "the lessons are over."

"Bwuthe wath wight," Wilfred said sadly. "Thir Winthton ith a dwopout."

CHAPTER NINE

THE very next day, Sir Winston dropped out of sight completely. When Ollie came home from school, Winnie's chain was empty. Not his collar, but his chain. It took a moment for this to register. Usually Winnie somehow managed to slip his collar and go hunting for porcupines and skunks.

But today the collar was gone and the fastener was not broken. Someone must have unsnapped the collar from the chain. To Ollie that could mean only one thing: Sir Winston had been stolen!

The news of Winnie's disappearance spread fast. In less than an hour, the yard was filled with his many admirers. By the time Chief Aldrich arrived on the scene, tires squealing and siren wailing, any chance of obtaining footprints had been erased.

After studying the situation and hearing Ollie's story, the chief gravely rendered his verdict. "As I see it," he announced, "Sir Winston has been stolen."

"Kidnapped," moaned Deedee.

"Dognapped," Bruce leered. "But don't worry, as soon as they get him under a strong light, they'll bring the homely mutt back."

"Bruce Dodge, how can you be so mean?" Deedee wailed.

"Oh, it's easy for him," Dusty said. "He was born that way."

Ollie looked at the chief hopefully. "We'll get him back, won't we, Chief Aldrich?" he asked.

With a reassuring smile, the chief clapped him on the shoulder. "I'm sure we will, Little Ollie," he said heartily. "My men and I will get him back quicker than you can say 'Sir Winston.' I'll go down to headquarters right now and issue an all-points bulletin."

Despite the fact that "headquarters" was a single small room in the town hall, and the chief's "men" consisted only of Tom Drury, a part-time officer, Ollie felt some better.

Until the chief turned as he was about to open the door of his cruiser. "By the way, Little Ollie, are you offering a reward? We have to specify. I might add it sometimes helps. Gives a little incentive, you know."

Ollie gulped. He had counted his money only last

night. After paying Winnie's obedience school tuition, he only had thirteen dollars and ninety-four cents left. Drat it! He sure wished he had that fifteen dollar tuition back. A lot of good it had done poor Winnie.

"Yes, there—there will be a reward," Ollie replied.

The chief whipped out his notebook and pencil. "How much shall I say?"

"Thirteen dollars and ninety-four cents," Ollie told him.

The chief looked up from his pad.

"Make that twenty-three dollars and ninety-four cents," Dusty piped up. "I have ten dollars in savings."

"Call it thirty-three dollars and ninety-four cents," Deedee added. "I have ten dollars, too."

"Forty-three dollars and ninety-four cents," Elmira joined in.

"Let's make it an even forty-four dollars," Bruce said. "I'll contribute six cents to the cause."

Everyone ignored him as others donated all they could to the reward. The chief's pencil was kept busy for a few minutes. When the last one had been heard from, he totaled the amount. "Well now, that's a sizable reward," he told them. "Comes to almost ninety dollars."

He looked around at the serious faces. "Tell you what *I'm* going to do. I'm going to up it to one hundred dollars. *That* should get some attention. We'll swing into action right away, Little Ollie. In the meantime, it wouldn't do any harm to put an ad in the lost and found column of the *Courier*."

Light flashing, siren wailing, tires squealing, Chief Aldrich shot out of the yard and down the street.

Ollie had already decided for himself to put an ad in the paper. He would spare no expense in tracking down his stolen pet. Accompanied by the whole Sir Winston fan club, Ollie descended on the newspaper office. They crowded into the room and found Nosy Newman on duty. Tall and lanky, Nosy covered sports for the weekly *Courier;* also births, deaths, social events, business, crime—and, on occasion, classified ads.

"Well, well, what goes on here?" Nosy greeted them. "From the sad looks on your faces, I'd say the school must have burned down."

Ollie shook his head. "Worse than that," he said mournfully. "Sir Winston has been stolen."

Nosy's eyes widened behind his horn-rimmed glasses. "You mean that big bulldog of yours—the team mascot?"

Ollie nodded solemnly. "Somebody just stole him right out of our yard."

Nosy reached for a pad and pencil. "And you want to put an ad in the lost and found—right?"

"Right," Ollie said.

Pencil poised, Nosy waited. "How do you want it worded?"

Ollie looked thoughtfully at the ceiling. "Mm-mmm. Lost, one brindle English bulldog. Big, handsome dog, weighs about fifty pounds." He paused and looked at the others.

"Answers to the name of either 'Sir Winston' or 'Winnie,' " Deedee added.

"Or 'mutt' or 'plug-ugly' or 'bowlegs' or 'hey, you,' " Bruce volunteered.

The others glared him into silence. "Generous reward being offered," Elmira put in.

Nosy wrote this all down. When he was through, Ollie asked hesitantly, "How—how much does it cost?"

"Well, let's see," Nosy said. "We charge by the word. That's one—two—three—"

"By the word?" Ollie said.

"By the word," Nosy replied. "One—two—three—"

"Uh, maybe we could cut a word here and there," Ollie ventured. "We want to keep that reward as high as we can."

"Everyone chipped in," Deedee said proudly. "We have a hundred dollars."

Nosy whistled. "That's a lot of chipping."

Ollie frowned at the ad Nosy had written down. Elmira, Deedee, Dusty and Bruce peered over his

shoulder. "We could take out 'one' and 'English'"
Ollie said. "That would make it, 'Lost brindle bulldog.'
We would save two words."

"Yeah," said Dusty. "They know it isn't ten bulldogs."

"And who cares whether he's English or Portu-
guese?" Bruce said.

"We could say, 'answers to name Sir Winston,'"
Elmira suggested. "If he answers to either name, all
we need is one of them."

"Hey, that's great," Ollie said. "We cut out 'the'
and 'of' and 'either' and 'or' and 'Winnie.' That's five
more words saved!"

Deedee clapped her hands. "And we could just
say, 'One hundred dollars reward.'"

Dusty looked at Nosy anxiously. "If we use the
numeral '$100' instead of the words 'one hundred
dollars,' would that count as one word instead of
three?"

Nosy thought it over carefully. "Well, here's what
we'll do," he finally said. "We'll run the ad just as you
gave it to me in the first place. You can keep the whole
hundred dollars for the reward. What's more, we're going to run that ad with a double hairline border on the
front page. How do you like that?"

Everyone liked it fine. Especially Ollie. It gave
him a warm feeling inside, the way Chief Aldrich and

all Winnie's friends and even Nosy Newman had rallied round in his hour of need. Ollie went home feeling very optimistic about the chances of finding Winnie.

When Mr. Scruggs and Mrs. Hunkins were told of the dognapping at supper, they were reassuring, too. "I'm sure he'll turn up," Mrs. Hunkins said.

"As far as I know, Chief Aldrich has never lost a stolen dog yet," Mr. Scruggs added.

As far as Ollie knew, Chief Aldrich had never *found* a stolen dog, either—for the very simple reason that no dog had ever been stolen in Willowdale. However, he felt the chief would be tireless in chasing down the criminal. And that ad on the front page of the *Courier* would alert the whole town. He would not want to be in that dog thief's shoes. He did not stand a chance of getting away with it!

Ollie went to sleep that night filled with confidence. In his dreams he and Winnie were reunited. . . .

In the days that followed, his confidence was a bit shaken. Chief Aldrich sent out his alert. The ad appeared on the front page of the *Courier,* double hairline border and all. The bicycle rodeo picture made the front page of the same issue. Nosy's candid shot of Ollie's bicycle on top of Ollie on top of the card table on top of a disheveled Mr. Waterhouse was the talk of the town. Only the loss of Winnie saved Ollie from possible disgrace.

But despite Chief Aldrich and the ad, the days dragged on with no sign of Winnie—nor even a clue to his whereabouts.

Not only was Ollie's confidence shaken, but that of the whole baseball team as well. Not having Winnie there as mascot seemed to affect their already shaky play. They lost to the Merchants on the following Tuesday night—a team that was tied with the Pirates for last place in the farm league. The Merchants walloped the Bulldogs 18 to 0.

"Let's face it," Deedee moaned after the game, "without our mascot we're nothing."

"When you come right down to it," Dusty said, "*with* him we haven't been too much lately."

And they were running out of games. There was only one left. On Thursday they would meet the Lisbon Lions in Lisbon. The Bulldogs still clung to a one-game lead. If they won, they would be farm league champions—with a good chance of making the regular Tom Thumb League next year.

But if they lost, the Bulldogs and Lions would be tied. There would be a play-off game in Willowdale on Saturday.

"If you guys beat the Lions tomorrow, I'll treat

you to as many sodas as you can hold," Rod Little promised them at practice on Wednesday night.

It would take more than a promise of ice cream sodas to fire up the Bulldogs, Ollie felt. If they were going to beat the Lions, more than anything else they needed to find Winnie.

CHAPTER TEN

WINNIE did not make the trip to Lisbon on Thursday. The Bulldogs had to take the field against the Lions without him.

There were several loyal fans on hand, however. Mr. Scruggs filled the car with Miss Carmody, Mrs. Hunkins, Deedee, Elmira and Wilfred to attend the championship game. For a farm league game, it excited a lot of interest.

Nosy Newman's timely shot of Ollie and Mr. Waterhouse on the front page of the *Courier* had made Ollie something of a local celebrity. The theft of Winnie, the team mascot, had brought the Bulldogs into the limelight, too. Nosy Newman was on hand today with his ever-ready camera.

"One thing you can be sure of," Ollie heard him tell Chief Aldrich, "wherever you find Ollie Scruggs, there is bound to be a lot of action."

There was not much action in the first inning. "Miller! Scruggs! Dodge!" Rod Little sang out, clapping his hands together. "Let's start this game off with some hits. But don't forget, Miller—the first man up in an inning takes a strike."

Dusty took three strikes and came trudging back to the bench, dragging his bat behind him.

Ollie did not fare much better. He did run the count to three and two before taking a futile cut at Bull Martin's fast ball.

"Man, that fast ball of his looks about as big as an aspirin today," he grumbled, joining Dusty on the bench.

"Yeah, only it *gives* you a headache, instead of curing one," Dusty replied.

"Just leave it up to Dodge," Bruce said confidently. "I'll take some of the steam out of him."

He did, too. He rifled one through the mound on the second pitch that made Bull Martin hit the dirt.

Shortstop Eddie Lane took the one-hopper in stride and nipped Bruce at first by a step to retire the side.

Dusty started the bottom half by walking the first

Lion to face him. "Let's talk it up out there," Rod called to the infielders.

The chatter erupted as Dusty faced Eddie Lane: "Easy out, old boy! Settle down, Dusty! Mow him down in there!"

Dusty did not mow Lane down. In fact, Lane mowed him down with a hot shot through the mound —just as Bruce had done to Bull Martin.

Shortstop Herbie Snell did not duplicate Lane's handling of Bruce's hit. This one tore the glove off his hand. By the time he retrieved it, a grinning Eddie Lane was perched on first.

"Lucky hit, Dusty!" Ollie yelled from right field. "You'll get the next one."

Little Max Shapiro hit a high infield fly between second and third that Herbie Snell took for the first out. Then Bull Martin stepped into the box. Martin's timely home runs were the main reason the Lions were still in this race.

Martin made Dusty pitch—taking him down to a full count and then fouling two off. On the next one, Martin connected. Playing deep in center field, Larry Donovan drifted back on the long fly, while Eddie Lane tagged up on first. Larry took the ball coming in and pegged to Herbie Snell at second, as Lane came charging down the baseline.

The ball was right in there. Herbie stuck his glove in front of the bag and Lane slid into it for the third out.

The Bulldog fans whistled and stamped their feet on the bleachers, in appreciation of the sparkling play.

"Nice going!" Rod praised them, when they came in for the top half of the second. "Snell! Martin! Turner! Let's go get 'em!"

The Bulldogs did not go get them in the second, third, or fourth inning. Neither did the Lions get to them—except for home runs by Bull Martin in the second and fourth, with no one on. Aside from that, Dusty traded the big Lion hurler out for out.

But going into the bottom half of the fifth, Dusty began to lose his stuff. They tagged him for a couple more runs.

Rod put a hand on Dusty's shoulder when he came in to the bench. "How are you doing, Miller?" he asked.

"I'm okay," Dusty assured him.

"Sure you're not getting tired?" Rod pressed. "I don't think you're throwing as hard as you were."

"He's throwing just as hard," Bruce said. "Trouble is, the ball is going slower. When they start reading the trademark on your fast ball as it goes by, it's time for a change."

Rod gave him a withering glance. "If you were

trying half as hard as Miller is, Dodge, this might be a different ball game. When you failed to back up third on that sacrifice bunt play, you cost us a run."

He turned to Ollie. "Speaking of which, *you* did not look like a winner last inning either, Scruggs. It's been a long time since I've seen anyone picked off with the hidden-ball trick. Let's be more alert—both of you!"

"Oh, they don't have to be alert," Dusty said, glaring at them. "After all, they're drones. Only us worker bees have to try."

This exchange spurred them on. Billy Young drew a base on balls. Larry Donovan, with a count of one and one, caught the next one with the end of his bat for a single into short right field. Two up, two on. The Bulldog fans began stomping their feet and chanting for another hit.

Dusty obliged by smashing a hard grounder to Eddie Lane at short, who bobbled it long enough to lose Dusty at first by a stride.

Now the Bulldog supporters were really talking it up. Bouncy and colorful in their white skirts and red sweaters, Deedee and Elmira sent a cheer ringing across the diamond: "One—two—three—four! Who —are—we—for! Ollie Scruggs! Ollie Scruggs! Ollie Scruggs!"

Still smarting under Rod's and Dusty's criticism,

Ollie strode to the plate, grimly determined to blast one out of the park. He took the first pitch. Ball one. The second was low for ball two. Ollie stepped out of the box and wiped his sweating palms on his pants.

The next one was right over. Ollie unwound and connected. Crack! It felt like a solid hit. The ball arched high over the infield—kept climbing over left fielder Max Shapiro. Going—going—

"Foul ball!" yelled the umpire.

The fans subsided with a groan. Shoulders slumped, Ollie picked up his bat and stepped back into the box. Rats! Now he had to do it all over again—only straighten it out.

Which was exactly what he did. Once again, Martin's pitch was in there. Again Ollie unwound and connected. Crack! The ball arched high over the infield— kept climbing over Max Shapiro. Going—going— gone! Fair by a yard!

Ollie basked in the warmth of the resounding cheers as he jogged around the bases. His teammates were standing in line to shake his hand when he crossed the plate.

The warmth was still there when he took his position in right field a short time later. Bull Martin had set his square jaw and mowed down three men in a row. But Ollie's grand slam homer had tied the game, 4 to 4. Now they had to hold the Lions in the bottom half of the sixth, then go on to beat them in extra innings for the championship.

"Let's salt 'em away—one, two three!" Rod urged them as they took the field.

The Bulldogs had no intention of letting the Lions score. Dusty set Eddie Lane down on three straight pitches. Then Max Shapiro banged Dusty for a triple, and Bull Martin stepped up to the plate. Two outs away from the championship. Ollie backed up in right field. Both of Martin's homers had gone over the right field fence.

"Let's have another one, Bull!" yelled the Lions' fans.

Dusty did not give him any chance. He served up three balls in a row. But the fourth one was where Martin could reach it—and he did. It was another long shot into right field.

Ollie turned and raced for the fence, with the crowd's hysterical screams in his ears. At the last moment, he leaped into the air and stuck out his glove. When he came down, the ball was in it. It was the thrill of his life.

"Scruggs—you nitwit! Scruggs—you dope! Scruggs—you drone!"

These were some of the unkind comments that reached Ollie's ears. Coming out of his dream world, where already he was being carried around the field on the shoulders of his adoring fans after an extra-inning victory, Ollie became aware of what he had done. With a runner on third and one out, he had caught a long foul! Max Shapiro had tagged up and was even now crossing the plate with the winning run.

"Never, I mean *never*, catch a long foul late in a game with the winning or tying run on third and less than two out."

Now this oft-repeated advice of Rod's came back to haunt Ollie. In his eagerness to catch the ball, he had not even thought that the ball might go foul.

Baseball sure was a funny game, Ollie thought. The object usually was to catch the ball if you could. But here was a case where he had lost the game because he had caught the ball.

Now they would have to meet the Lions in Willowdale on Saturday in a play-off for the championship.

CHAPTER ELEVEN

OLLIE's teammates were not very friendly the next day. On Friday, the gang usually went to the Willowdale Pharmacy for a snack. Today, they went along without him. And when he got there, they were nowhere to be seen.

Ollie found an empty booth and ordered a banana split. When it came and he began eating it, he could hear someone talking in the booth next to the one where he was sitting. Ollie could not see who it was because a high partition separated the booths.

At first, he did not pay much attention—not until he heard his name mentioned. "Well, I hope he's satisfied," the voice was saying. "Ollie sure has changed lately. He's so lazy around the house, he doesn't even mow the lawn any more. Before Winnie was stolen, he didn't feed him half the time—Mrs. Hunkins had to. Rod Little tells us something a dozen times and Ollie doesn't even bother to listen. So he's such a drone he goes and costs us the big game—maybe even the championship!"

Ollie recognized that voice all too well. After all, he heard it practically every day of his life, didn't he? It belonged to Dusty. And Dusty had been his best friend from as far back as he could remember.

Or so he had thought. Tears stung Ollie's eyelids as he sat there, listening. It hurt to swallow. He felt all choked up. That was his first reaction: a sick feeling inside to catch his best friend talking about him behind his back. To his face—okay. But not behind his back!

Then Ollie got angry. That was his second reaction: to jump to his feet and face Dusty. He would call Dusty a traitor and walk out. Then he would never speak to Dusty again as long as he lived. But he could not do that. No, what he should do was slip out quietly. He would never even mention this. He would go on as though nothing had happened. But things would never be the same between Dusty and him. Not ever again. As far as he was concerned, they were no longer best friends.

Come to think of it, he did not have any friends

now, Ollie thought on the way home. He swallowed hard, thinking of man's best friend—Winnie. Where was he? Ollie wondered. Were they taking good care of him? Were—were they feeding him enough? Winnie had a big appetite. Not that Ollie, the drone, had spent much time feeding Winnie before he was stolen. But he knew Mrs. Hunkins had been taking care of it—she was a worker bee.

When would there be a break in the dognapping? Ollie wondered.

It came the very next morning. Ollie was sitting on the back steps after breakfast, chin in hands, when Dusty appeared on the scene, eating a doughnut. "You look as if you had lost your best friend," Dusty greeted him.

Ollie stiffened, but said nothing. If Dusty only knew! Ollie was staring sadly at Winnie's empty chain. It lay right where the thief had left it, when he stole Winnie. Ollie could not bring himself to touch it.

"Any leads yet?" Dusty inquired.

Ollie shook his head without speaking, or even lifting his chin from his hands.

"Sure beats all," Dusty said, sitting down beside Ollie. "With Chief Aldrich on the case, and that ad on the front page of the *Courier*, wouldn't you think they'd find a clue?"

Before Ollie could reply, Deedee came skipping

around the corner. "Mom wants you to go down to Harry's Market and charge a dozen eggs, a loaf of bread, and two pounds of hamburg," she notified her brother. "Her supply of hamburg patties in the freezer is getting low again. She wants to make up some more to have on hand."

"Do you have a fractured ankle or something?" Dusty said.

"I got two pounds of hamburg for her yesterday," Deedee said primly. "Now it's your turn."

"Oh, all right," Dusty said, getting reluctantly to his feet. "But it seems to me I just got two pounds for her yesterday or the day before, too. What's she doing —keeping a tiger in the kitchen?"

He looked at Ollie. "How about coming with me? We can talk about the game this afternoon."

In keeping with his vow to go on as though he had not heard Dusty talking about him yesterday, Ollie went along. When they got to the market, Harry greeted Dusty's order with a chuckle. He was a moon-faced, pink-cheeked man whose stomach jiggled when he laughed. "My, we're having quite a run on hamburg at your house these days, aren't we? Your father picked up two pounds last night. Deedee got two pounds yesterday morning, you got two pounds the day before, your mother picked up two pounds the same day when she was shopping, Wilfred just charged two pounds this morning—and now you want two pounds more."

He shook his head. "I hate to spoil a good thing, but you'd better tell your mother that she should buy a cow at a time, instead of a pound."

When Ollie and Dusty got back to Dusty's house, Dusty told his mother exactly what Harry had told him. She smiled as she made patties and put them in plastic bags. "I must say we do seem to be using a lot of hamburg these days. But I had no idea we were using *that* much. Your father must have noticed the supply was low and picked up two pounds without telling me. And as to Wilfred—"

She broke off and looked intently at Dusty. "Are you *sure* he said Wilfred charged two pounds?"

"Yes, Mom—I'm positive," Dusty assured her. "Didn't he, Ollie?"

Ollie nodded vigorously.

"Hmmm," Mrs. Miller said thoughtfully. "What in the world would Wilfred do that for? And why so many hamburg patties? Anyone would think we were supplying a dog kennel with—"

The same thought struck all of them at once.

"Do you suppose—" Mrs. Miller left it unfinished.

"Don't tell me he's the one—" Dusty did, too.

"—who took Winnie!" Ollie blurted it out.

"Speaking of Wilfred—here he comes up the walk

now," Mrs. Miller said, slipping the patties into the freezer. She put a finger to her lips. "Shh. Let's step into the living room and see what he does."

What Wilfred did was to go directly to the freezer and peer into it. With a grunt of satisfaction, he reached in and took out the patties. Slipping them under his gray sweatshirt, he scurried out of the house. In the yard, he paused briefly, looked furtively in all directions, then made a beeline across the playground and melted into the pine forest beyond.

Mrs. Miller, Dusty and Ollie were not far behind. Ollie was amazed at how nimble Mrs. Miller was as the three sleuths flitted from tree to tree. In a short time, they came to the old "Cross Place," where the farmhouse had long since gone to ruin, but the barn was still standing.

Mrs. Miller, Dusty and Ollie remained hidden behind trees. "Let's wait just a minute and see what happens," Mrs. Miller suggested.

What happened was that Wilfred emerged from the barn—with Winnie walking sedately at his side on a leash! Sir Winston remained at Wilfred's left side in perfect heel position as Wilfred walked in a big circle.

Ollie would have burst out of the woods with a yelp of joy and relief if Mrs. Miller had not laid a restraining hand on his arm. "Look he's training Winnie!" she whispered.

Ollie looked, and sure enough, Wilfred was putting on quite a show. There was a choke collar around Winnie's neck, but Wilfred did not seem to need it much. Completing his circle, Wilfred came to a halt, and so did Winnie.

"Thir Winthton—thit!" Wilfred commanded firmly.

Sir Winston sat. He did not sit crooked, either.

"Well, I'll be jiggered—straight as a string!" Ollie said.

"Exerthithe finithed—praithe your dog!" Wilfred told himself.

Whereupon he took the plastic bag of hamburg patties from under his sweatshirt, peeled one off and held it out. "Good dog," Wilfred said, patting Winnie on the head.

Sir Winston inhaled the patty like a vacuum cleaner sucking in a fly.

Resuming his "attitude of command," Wilfred cried out, "Thtay!" Dropping the leash to the ground, he walked forward several steps. Sir Winston remained in sitting position.

Dusty picked this particular moment to sneeze. Sir Winston never twitched a muscle, but Wilfred did.

He headed for the woods in the opposite direction as fast as his short legs would carry him. Mrs. Miller overtook him in just a few steps and swept him off his feet.

"Ollie didn't want Winnie, tho I took him!" Wilfred sobbed. "He didn't feed him or make him mind or—or anything. He ith a dwone!"

They finally got him calmed down and headed for home. Ollie thought about what Wilfred had said all the way back—that he was a drone.

"You can be a drone, too, if you want to be," he had told Winnie. "It's a lot easier than being a worker bee."

A lot easier, maybe—but was it much fun? What fun was it to have everyone think you were lazy? What fun was it to lose your dog because you did not take good care of him?

"Drones have their place, but it's the worker bees who get things done," his father had said. "No worker bees—no hive."

"No worker bees—no honey," Mrs. Hunkins had added.

And no worker bees—no farm league championship, Ollie admitted.

Ollie's ears burned as he recalled Dusty's words: "I hope he's satisfied . . . Rod Little tells us something a dozen times and Ollie doesn't even bother to listen. So he's such a drone he goes and costs us the big game—maybe even the championship."

Ollie's jaw set grimly. No, he was not satisfied. He would not be satisfied until he made Dusty Miller sorry for what he had said behind Ollie's back.

And Ollie intended to do just that in the play-off game against Lisbon this afternoon!

CHAPTER TWELVE

CHIEF Aldrich was relieved when he was notified about Winnie. Five minutes after Mrs. Miller called him, he pulled into the yard, siren wailing—followed by half a dozen youngsters—Bruce, Deedee and Elmira included.

Eyes twinkling, the chief winked at Ollie when all the details had been learned. "Well now, I guess the case is closed, Little Ollie—unless you want to press charges."

Both Dusty and Deedoo jumped in front of Wilfred protectingly. "No, no, you can't do that!" Dusty protested.

"He's just a little boy!" Deedee said.

Wilfred beamed with pleasure to find that he had such staunch defenders. "Only five yearth old," he announced.

Ollie shook his head. "I wouldn't do that," he told Chief Aldrich. "In fact, I might even give him my thirteen dollars and ninety-four cents for a reward. He taught Winnie a lot." Grinning sheepishly, he added, "and I learned something, too."

"Make that fourteen dollars even," Bruce offered. "I'll kick in six cents for what I learned." He looked at Ollie disgustedly. "Something tells me that you can't make a drone out of a worker bee."

Dusty sniffed. "Any more than you can make a worker bee out of a drone."

Elmira clucked. "Don't try to fool me, Bruce Dodge," she said. "I saw you practicing hard on your bicycle before the rodeo. And you did not get one hundred on that test by reading comic books. You're not all drone."

Bruce flushed in embarrassment. "Oh, go practice your cartwheels, Elmira Busybee," he said. "We want to talk baseball."

"Hey, that's right," Dusty said. "We have a game to play this afternoon."

It still hurt Ollie to think that Dusty would talk about him behind his back. Ollie knew those remarks would always hurt. A friend was supposed to be someone you could trust. Now, after all these years, Dusty was no longer a good friend.

Ollie looked at Dusty accusingly. "We're going to win the game, too—even with Scruggs, the drone, playing in right field."

Apparently a lot of other people thought the Bulldogs would win. The Willowdale stands were filled with students and townspeople that afternoon.

Even Miss Hall was there. When she saw Ollie march across the field to the Bulldog bench with Sir Winston in step at his side, she came to offer congratulations. "I see you took my advice, Oliver," she said. "I am looking forward to having you and Sir Winston back in class."

While Ollie was pleased by all this praise, he would not be surprised if Winnie's good behavior were temporary. Winnie had a long-standing grudge against skunks, porcupines and other dogs. That would be hard to overcome permanently.

"I helped twain him," Wilfred spoke up.

Miss Hall patted him on the head. "I'm sure you did, Wilfred. Some day you will make a fine dog twainer—I mean trainer."

Instead of crawling under the bench for a snooze, Winnie, held on his leash by Wilfred, sat on his haunches and watched what was going on.

What he saw was a pitcher's duel between Billy Young and Max Shapiro for five innings. No hits, no runs, no errors—not even by Ollie.

It was largely due to Ollie that the Lions did not score. He chased down fly balls out there in right field until he was panting. Half a dozen times the crowd applauded his spectacular catches.

Playing first base, Dusty was moved to praise him when they took the field for the top of the sixth inning. "You're doing a great job, Ollie," he said.

Ollie ignored him and trotted on toward right field.

Eddie Lane opened the inning by watching two strikes go by. Then he smashed a grounder to Herbie Snell at short, which Herbie zipped to first for the out.

Shapiro stepped into the box and faced Billy. Billy's fast ball was still hopping, and Max missed two of them in a row. Then he got a piece of one for a foul ball. The next pitch he bounced off the fence in left field for a triple, and the Lion fans had something to cheer about.

Especially with Bull Martin coming up to bat. As he moved back in right field, Ollie was reminded of Bruce's remark before the game.

"How do you pitch to Martin?" Billy Young had asked Dusty's advice.

"With your fingers crossed," Bruce had butted in. "But come to think of it, I did notice on Thursday that Martin has one weakness."

Billy turned to him eagerly. "What's that?"

"He can only hit home runs right-handed," Bruce replied.

Well, Ollie decided, Martin was not going to hit one today, if he could help it. And Martin did not waste much time before trying. He belted Billy's first pitch deep into right field. Sure that Martin's hit would go for extra bases, Max Shapiro legged it for home. He was almost there when a roar from the crowd told him that Ollie had made a running one-hand catch. Shapiro beat it back to third to tag up and once again sprinted for the plate.

When Ollie turned to throw, he found that the whole Bulldog infield was in proper position, for a change. Les Martin had raced over from second to act as relay. Dusty was down near home plate to cut off Les's peg, if necessary. Billy was backing up Mike Turner behind home plate.

It was a precision play. Ollie's throw to Les was right in the groove. Les wheeled and let fly toward Dusty. It was Mike's job to direct the play, and he did. "Let it go!" he yelled at Dusty.

Dusty stepped away from the throw at the last moment and the ball spat into Mike's mitt on one hop.

He set himself and tagged Max sliding into the plate. The Lion threat was snuffed out.

"Now you're playing baseball!" Rod praised them with a pleased grin.

"Beautiful play, Ollie," Dusty said. "You saved us a run—maybe two."

Without a word, Ollie turned and picked up his favorite brown bat.

"Okay, Donovan—Miller—Scruggs!" Rod called out. "Let's wrap it up!"

That was just what he was going to do, Ollie determined.

Max Shapiro's fast ball was still hopping, too. He used it to retire Larry Donovan on three straight pitches. The Willowdale crowd groaned.

"Come on, Dusty, let's have a hit," Mike Turner chattered. "Remember those ice cream sodas! All you can eat!"

Dusty did not smile. He was grim as he rubbed dirt on his hands and stepped in there to face Shapiro. One pitch, and he was standing on second base with a solid double.

Now it was Ollie's turn to be grim. The Bulldog supporters were chanting for action. Deedee and Elmira led the crowd in a cheer: "Extra, extra, read all about it! Ollie's going to hit, and there's no doubt about it!"

There was no doubt in Ollie's mind. He stood there with his bat cocked, waiting for the one he wanted. It was not the first pitch—too wide, for ball one. It was not the second one, either—even though it caught the outside corner for a strike. Nor was it the next one—an inside pitch that moved him back in a hurry.

"Strike two!" Umpire Chief Aldrich yelled.

Ollie could not help but glance at the chief questioningly.

"It was right in there, Little Ollie," Chief Aldrich assured him.

Ollie wiped his hands and stepped back in. Now Max Shapiro had him in a hole. Shapiro would probably waste a couple—and he did. The count went to three and two. Max could not waste any more.

Although that last pitch was still not the one that Ollie wanted, he decided it would have to do. It was probably a ball, but Ollie would not settle for a walk.

It was high and outside—but Ollie went fishing for it. He caught it, too—with the fat of his bat. Smack! It felt like a solid hit. With great satisfaction, he saw Vern Libby race deep into center field. He saw the ball clear the fence for a home run. As he turned the corner at first, he saw Dusty cross home plate with the winning run.

They were all standing in line to shake his hand

when he came jogging in. There was his father with Miss Carmody and Mrs. Hunkins. There was Deedee and Elmira and Wilfred. There was Rod and Billy and Mike—and even Bruce. There was Winnie barking a greeting.

Last of all, there was Dusty with his hand outstretched. "Nice going," he said with a smile. "I knew you could do it *if* you got on the ball."

Ollie had laughed at this once, but not this time. Now that the game was all over, he felt kind of drained and empty. He missed being friends. But he still remembered what Dusty had said about him in the Willowdale Pharmacy yesterday. He would not have minded if Dusty had lectured him to his face. But to have Dusty discuss his faults with someone else—

Strangely enough, Dusty's smile widened into a broad grin. "I guess that *was* kind of a mean trick I played on you, pal. But it worked."

Ollie's brown eyes widened. "What trick?"

Dusty shrugged. "Yesterday in the drugstore I slipped into the booth next to you and said all those things on purpose. But I was all alone in the booth. I wanted to get you angry. You—you're not cut out to be a drone."

Ollie just stood there and stared at Dusty. A wave of guilt swept over him. If Dusty had not stung him into action, he knew he never would have played as he had today.

"You know what?" Ollie said.

Dusty cocked his blond head. "What?"

Ollie laughed. "I don't think I am, either," he agreed.

It was good to be laughing again with his friend. His very best friend. The best friend in the world.